PRETTY KITTY

With admiration for my friend Helene,
who has rescued more kitties than I can count!
—K. B.

For my dear Rez and sweetest little Fritzy—
one wonderful man and his very special kitty
—S. L.

Henry Holt and Company, *Publishers since 1866*
175 Fifth Avenue, New York, NY 10010 · mackids.com

Henry Holt® is a registered trademark of Macmillan Publishing Group, LLC
Text copyright © 2018 by Karen Beaumont
Illustrations copyright © 2018 by Stephanie Laberis
All rights reserved.

Library of Congress Control Number: 2017957922
ISBN 978-0-8050-9232-5

Our books may be purchased in bulk for promotional, educational, or business use.
Please contact your local bookseller or the Macmillan Corporate and Premium Sales Department
at (800) 221-7945 ext. 5442 or by e-mail at MacmillanSpecialMarkets@macmillan.com.

Printed in China by Hung Hing Off-set Printing Co., Ltd.,
Heshan City, Guangdong Province

First edition, 2018 / Designed by Liz Dresner
The illustrations for this book were created digitally.

1 3 5 7 9 10 8 6 4 2

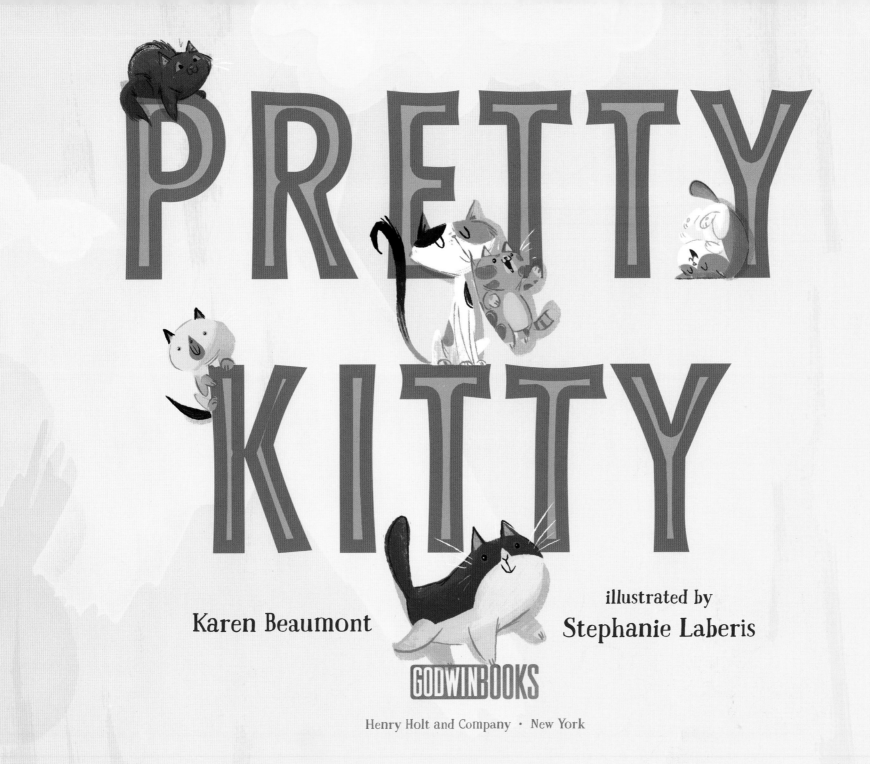

PRETTY
KITTY

Karen Beaumont

illustrated by
Stephanie Laberis

GODWINBOOKS

Henry Holt and Company · New York

Old man.

Big city.

STACIA'S GROCERY

144th

8th

Pretty kitty.
Pretty little itty-bitty
kitty cat.

Pretty kitty. Wants a pat.
Don't you look at me like that.
I do not want a kitty cat.

SCAT!

2 kitties on the mat,
Don't you look at me like that.
I do not want a kitty cat.

Mercy me! Now they're **THREE**.
No, you can't move in with me.

Might have FLEAS

Or some DISEASE.

Think you might be SIAMESE.

3 kitties on the mat,
Don't you look at me like that.
I do not want a kitty cat.

SCAT!

TWO, FOUR,

There's one more
Kitty scratching at my door.

Sakes alive!
There are **FIVE**.
Just don't know
if I'd survive. . . .

Might be mean. Might even bite.
Probably start a kitty fight.

Keep this old man
up all night.

5 kitties on the mat,
Don't you look at me like that.
I do not want a kitty cat.

SCAT!

Oh, brother,
Not another!
Looks like she may be the mother.

So scrawny. Here's a scrap.
No, you can't get on my lap!

6 kitties on the mat,
Please don't look at me like that.
I do not want a kitty cat.

SCAT!

No, no!
Down you go!

Achoo! Sneeze, sneeze!
Oh, my gosh! My allergies!

7 kitties on the mat,
Please don't look at me like that.
I do not want a kitty cat.

SCAT!

Hope you're tame.
What's your name?
No, my answer's still the same.
8 kitties on the mat,
Please don't look at me like that.
I do not want a kitty cat.
SCAT!

9 kitties on the mat,
Please don't look at me like that.
I do not want a kitty cat.

SCAT!

Not again!
Now they're **TEN**.

Kitties cry. Very sly.
Time for you to say good-bye.

Oh, no!

Starts to snow.

You must have somewhere
else to go.

Somewhere.

Anywhere.

Can't say that
I really care . . .

... much.

10 kitties on the mat,
Please don't look at me like that.
I do not want a kitty cat.

SCAT!

Old man.

Big city.

Loves each pretty little kitty.

For Zac and India —K.B.

For Kate —G.H.

mackids.com

Library of Congress Cataloging-in-Publication Data
Banks, Kate, 1960–
    The bear in the book / Kate Banks ; pictures by Georg Hallensleben. — 1st ed.
        p.   cm.
    Summary: At the end of the day a little boy falls asleep as his mama reads
about a bear hibernating.
    ISBN 978-0-374-30591-8
    [1. Bedtime—Fiction.   2. Reading—Fiction.   3. Bears—Fiction.
4. Hibernation—Fiction.]   I. Hallensleben, Georg, ill.   II. Title.

PZ7.B22594Bea 2012
[E]—dc23
                                                              2011036691

The Bear in the Book

Kate Banks

Pictures by **Georg Hallensleben**

Frances Foster Books / Farrar Straus Giroux / New York

Once there was a book.
It was square, with words and colorful pictures.
And it lived on a shelf with many other books.
It belonged to a little boy and it was his favorite book.

When it was time for a story,
the boy took the book from the shelf.
He opened it and looked at the pictures.
Then he handed the book to his mama.
She spread it across her lap.
The boy cuddled up next to her.

The book was about a big black bear who went to sleep for the winter.

"Do bears really sleep all winter long?" asked the boy.

"Yes," his mother said. "They hibernate."

The boy turned the page.

The bear was munching on berries and leaves.

He was fattening himself up for the winter.

Then he gathered twigs and carried them to his den.

"He is making a soft bed," said the boy's mother.

The boy turned the page.

The bear had curled himself up into a ball.

He was bedding down where he would stay until spring.

"Sleep, big black bear," said the boy's mother.

"Shh," said the boy.

Snowflakes began to fall across the pages of the book.
The snow sat snugly in the boughs of the trees.
The boy could almost feel it.
"Snow is cold," he said. He nestled closely against his mother.
"I like snow," he said.

"Winter settled like a big hush," read the boy's mother.
"And the big black bear slept."
"Shh," said the boy.

Life went on outside the bear's den.
Rabbits hopped through the snowdrifts.
The trees shivered.
And the wind blew its icy breath across the fields.
The boy found the animals hidden in the pictures.
A deer, a rabbit, and a fox.

Then he pointed to the children gliding across the ice.
"The lake froze into a frosty mirror," read his mother.
"I'd like to skate," said the boy.
"When you're bigger," said his mother.

The boy touched the sharp corners of the book.
Then he climbed onto his mama's lap.
He felt the soft cotton of her shirt.
She wrapped her arms around him.
And she turned the page.

The sun was shining above the forest.

"Yellow," said the boy, smiling at its bright round face.

"Blue," he said, touching the sky.

"Red," said Mama, pointing to a pair of mittens.

"And black," said the boy, pointing to the sleeping bear.

"Sleep, big black bear," said his mother.

Along came a rumbling snowplow.
Someone chopped wood for a fire.
But the bear did not wake.

Mama turned the page again.
Smoke spiraled from chimneys writing messages across the sky.
"In the house is a warm fire, a table, a chair, and a bed,"
read the boy's mama.

"My bed is warm, too," said the boy, yawning.
His eyes began to feel heavy.

Now he turned the page.
The trees had shrugged the snow off their backs.
Winter had crept off like a weary visitor.
But the big black bear was still sleeping.
"Shh," said Mama, turning another page.

Crocuses popped up through the earth.
A fox drank from a pond.
"I'm thirsty," said the little boy.
His mother got him a glass of water.
The boy held the book. He listened to the sound
the pages made when he turned them back and forth.
"Shh," he said to the sleeping bear.

The boy drank his water.

"Do you think the bear gets thirsty?" he asked.

"No," answered his mother. "He doesn't eat or drink the whole winter."

"He must be hungry when he wakes up," said the boy.

His mother nodded. "He is very hungry," she said. "And very thin."

The boy leaned his head on his mama's shoulder.

She turned to the last page of the book.
The bear was rolling over in his den.
The warm wind was tickling his back.
Spring had arrived.
"Wake up, big black bear, wake up," said the boy's mama.

The bear got to his feet.
He crossed the page.
And walked out into the sunshine.
But the boy's eyes had closed.

Now the little boy was sleeping. His mama tucked him into bed.
She closed the book and kissed him good night.
"Sleep, little boy, sleep," she said.